JUST
A LITTLE
DIFFERENT

BY GINA AND MERCER MAYER

For
Christina Dumas

🌷 **A GOLDEN BOOK • NEW YORK**

Golden Books Publishing Company, Inc., New York, New York 10106

A new critter moved into a house in my
neighborhood. His name is Zack. His family is
just a little different than the rest of the families
on our block, because his father is a turtle and
his mother is a rabbit.

My family and I went to visit Zack and his family.
They were very friendly, but Zack was a little shy.

Later, at baseball practice, I said to the critters,
"Let's ask Zack to join our team."

But the other critters didn't want to.
One of them said, "He's just too different to
be on our team."

That made me mad. I told Mom and Dad.
Mom said, "Being different is good. Our
differences make us special."

I decided Zack wasn't too different to be my
friend. I went over to ask him to come and play
at my house. His mom said he could.

Playing with Zack was fun. We made some big buildings. Then we made ourselves into big monsters who could knock the buildings down.

When I went to Zack's house, he showed me his computer. We drew some cool pictures on it for our moms.

Zack and I liked playing the same things. We played video games.

We played hide-and-seek from my sister.

We rode our bikes.

We even played cowboys.
I told my friends that Zack was a
lot of fun.

But they still thought he was just too different.
One of the critters made fun of Zack. That really
made me mad.

One day Zack and I decided to build a clubhouse. We got some scraps of wood and some tools.

Zack's dad helped us.

While we were working, some of the critters walked by.

"What are you doing?" they asked. We told them.

They thought it was so cool that they wanted to join our club, too.

Zack said they could.

We worked on the clubhouse all day. We all had
fun together.

When the clubhouse was finished, we had our first club meeting. We decided that Zack should be club leader, since the clubhouse was in his yard.

And the other critters asked Zack to be on our baseball team.
He plays first base.

Now Zack is one of the gang.
It doesn't matter to anyone that he's just a little different. He's the most popular critter in the neighborhood.

But I'm still his best friend.